Wild Tales of the Unexplained

The Short Story Collection

"For the ones who love to imagine the unknown, the could be..." - Robert Tiller

Finding Love in All the Right Spaces

Samantha had always been a curious and adventurous person, so when she saw a strange object hovering in the sky one evening, she couldn't resist the urge to investigate. She climbed into her car and followed the object until it landed in a field just outside of town.

As she approached the strange, glowing craft, she was suddenly overcome by a feeling of calm and peacefulness. She felt herself being lifted off the ground and into the air, and the next thing she knew, she was inside the alien ship.

At first, Samantha was terrified. She had heard stories of people being abducted by aliens and never being seen again, and she had no idea what was happening to her. But as she looked into the eyes of her captor, a tall, slender being with shimmering skin and piercing blue eyes, she felt a strange sense of familiarity.

Over the next few days, Samantha and the alien, whom she learned was named Zarek, spent every moment together, talking and exploring the ship. As they got to know each other, Samantha realized that she had fallen in love with Zarek.

When it was time for Zarek to return to his home planet, Samantha knew that she couldn't stay behind. She begged Zarek to take her with him, and to her surprise, he agreed.

As they flew through the stars together, Samantha knew that she had found her true soulmate in the most unexpected of places. She knew that their love would continue to grow, no matter where their journey took them. Would you have went for it?

The All-American Hero

John had always been a tough, no-nonsense kind of guy, and he wasn't about to let a bunch of aliens kidnap him without a fight. When he saw the strange, glowing craft hovering over his ranch one evening, he knew he had to take action.

Grabbing his trusty rifle, John ran outside and aimed it at the ship. As the aliens emerged from the craft, he saw that they were tall, slender beings with shimmering skin and piercing eyes. They looked like something straight out of a sci-fi movie, but John wasn't about to let them get the best of him.

He fired off round after round, determined to take down every last one of the aliens. The creatures screeched and fell to the ground, one by one, as John's bullets found their mark.

When the last of the aliens lay motionless on the ground, John stood tall, panting and covered in sweat. He had fought off an entire horde of extraterrestrial invaders, and he had done it all on his own.

As he looked down at the defeated aliens, John couldn't help but feel a sense of pride. He was a man who would stop at nothing to protect what was his, and he knew that no one could mess with him and get away with it.

In that moment, John knew that he was a hero, and he would always be ready to defend his home and his loved ones, no matter what threats came his way.

An Out of This World Type of Family

I was scared at first when the aliens came for me. I had heard stories about people being taken by strange, otherworldly beings, and I had no idea what was happening. But as I looked into the eyes of the aliens, I saw kindness and compassion there, and I knew that they meant me no harm.

They lifted me off the ground and into the air, and before I knew it, I was inside their ship. I was amazed by all the strange and wonderful things I saw there - machines and devices that I had never even dreamed of.

The aliens were so kind to me, and they did everything they could to make me feel comfortable. They told me that they had been watching me for a long time, and they had seen the way my parents treated me. They said that they couldn't bear to see me suffer any longer, and that's why they had taken me with them.

At first, I was confused and a little bit scared. But as I got to know the aliens better, I realized that they were just like me - they wanted to be loved and to feel safe. And as I spent more time with them, I began to see that they were my friends, and that they would always be there for me.

Now, I am happy and safe with the aliens, and I know that they will never let anyone hurt me again. They have become my family, and I am grateful to them for taking me away from my abusive home.

Con-man of the Stars

George had always been a bit of a con man, and he had always had a knack for finding ways to make a quick buck. So when he saw the strange, otherworldly being wandering through the junkyard where he worked, he knew he had an opportunity to make a sale.

The alien, who looked like something out of a sci-fi movie, was searching for a car that could take him back to his home planet. George saw his chance and led the alien to a beat-up old Buick, claiming that it was a special, one-of-a-kind spacecraft that could fly to the stars.

The alien, who was desperate to get home, was eager to believe George's lies, and he agreed to buy the Buick on the spot. George couldn't believe his luck - he had just made a fortune selling a junker to an alien!

As the alien prepared to take off in his new "spacecraft," George couldn't help but feel a pang of guilt. He knew that the Buick would never be able to fly, and that the alien would be stuck on Earth forever.

But it was too late to turn back now, and George watched as the alien climbed into the Buick and took off into the sky. He knew that he had made a mistake, and he couldn't help but wonder what would have happened if the alien had bought a Delorean instead.

As the Buick disappeared into the clouds sputtering and breaking down, George realized that he had let his greed get the best of him, and he vowed to be more honest in the future. But for the alien, it was too late - he was now stuck on Earth, far from home. The car broke down...

Friends Don't Let Friends Get Abducted

Harold, Ronnie, and Hermione were out on a routine foosball practice when they saw something strange in the sky. It was a bright, glowing object that seemed to be moving closer and closer to them.

Before they knew it, the object had landed on the pitch, and a group of aliens emerged from the ship. They were tall, slender beings with shimmering skin and piercing eyes, and they seemed to be looking for something.

The aliens didn't waste any time - they grabbed Harold and lifted him off the ground, pulling him into the ship. Ronnie and Hermione watched in horror as Harold was taken away, not knowing what to do.

But they knew that they had to act fast if they wanted to save their friend. They raced back to the castle and grabbed their trusty flying automobile, determined to follow the aliens and bring Harold back home.

As they flew through the air, Ronnie and Hermione knew that they were up against some pretty formidable foes. But they were determined to save Harold, and they weren't about to let a few aliens stand in their way.

When they finally caught up to the aliens' ship, they saw that Harold was being held captive in a strange, alien chamber. They knew they had to act fast, so they used all their wizarding skills to break him free and escape back to Earth.

In the end, they managed to save the day and bring Harold home safe and sound. And they knew that they could always count on each other, no matter what dangers lay ahead.

What's Really Inside Area 51?

For years, people had whispered about the strange goings-on at Area 51 - the mysterious government facility in the Nevada desert. Some said that it was a top-secret testing ground for advanced military technology, while others claimed that it was a hideout for aliens and their spacecraft.

No one knew for sure what was really happening at Area 51, but one thing was certain - no one was allowed to get close to the facility. It was guarded by armed soldiers and surrounded by miles of barren desert, and anyone who tried to breach the perimeter was quickly turned away.

But as it turned out, all of the rumors were true. Deep beneath the surface of Area 51, there was a hidden tunnel that led to an underground world where aliens from all over the universe had made their home.

The aliens had been living in the tunnel for centuries, and they had built a thriving, technologically advanced society there. They had everything they needed to live and thrive - food, water, and all the resources they could ask for.

But as the years went by, the aliens began to grow curious about the surface world. They knew that humans lived up there, and they wanted to learn more about them. So they sent out a team of explorers to investigate, and they were amazed by what they found.

The aliens were fascinated by the humans and their way of life, and they knew that they had to find a way to make contact. So they began to send messages to the humans, hoping that one day, they would be able to meet and learn from each other.

And so, the secret of Area 51 was finally revealed, and the humans and the aliens began to work together, building a brighter, more connected future for all of them.

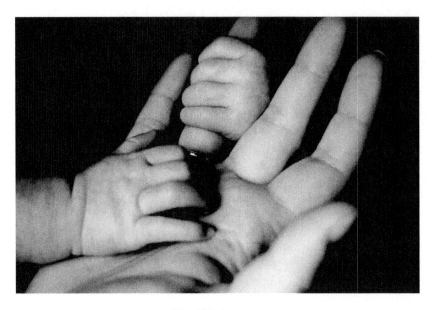

My Baby Alien

The alien baby was just a few days old when he was left behind on Earth. His parents had been on a mission to explore the planet, and they had accidentally left him behind when they returned to their home world.

The baby was alone and abandoned, with no way to get back to his own planet. He was discovered by a tribe of jungle people, who took him in and raised him as one of their own.

The baby grew quickly, and as he grew, he began to exhibit strange powers and abilities that the jungle people had never seen before. He could communicate with animals and control the elements, and he seemed to be connected to the natural world in a way that no one else was.

As he grew older, the alien baby became a powerful leader among the jungle people. He used his powers to protect his adopted tribe, and he became a notorious king who ruled their land for hundreds of years.

The people loved and revered their king, and they knew that he was a gift from the stars. They were grateful to him for bringing prosperity and peace to their land, and they knew that they would always be loyal to him, no matter what challenges lay ahead.

Not Your Typical Musician

The alien had always dreamed of living on Earth, and he had spent years studying the human race, learning everything he could about their culture and their way of life. When he finally had the chance to become a human himself, he jumped at the opportunity.

Through a series of celestial rights changes, the alien was able to become certified as a real human on his own planet. And when the time was right, he was transplanted into Earth's society, taking on a new identity as a musician.

No one on Earth knew the true identity of the musician - they just knew that he was a mysterious, otherworldly figure who could create magic with his music. He toured the world, playing to sold-out crowds and winning hearts wherever he went.

As the years went by, the alien became a household name, and people everywhere knew his music. But no one knew the truth about his past, or about the journey that had brought him to Earth.

And that was just the way the alien liked it - he enjoyed his anonymity and his freedom, and he knew that he would always be able to make his mark on the world through his music.

The Homemade Spaceship

As a child, Tommy was always fascinated by space. He spent hours staring up at the stars, dreaming of what it would be like to travel to the far reaches of the universe.

One night, Tommy couldn't take it anymore - he had to see what was out there for himself. So he snuck out of his house and made his way to the garage, where he set to work building a UFO out of household items.

It wasn't easy - Tommy had to use all of his creativity and resourcefulness to cobble together a spacecraft that was sturdy enough to withstand the rigors of space travel. But after hours of hard work, he finally had a functional UFO, and he was ready to take to the skies.

As Tommy flew through the air, he felt a sense of exhilaration that he had never experienced before. The wind whipped through his hair as he soared through the night sky, and he knew that he was living his dream.

And then, as he flew higher and higher, he saw something that he never could have imagined. A group of aliens, shining brightly in the darkness, appeared before him.

The aliens were friendly and welcoming, and they mistook Tommy for one of their own. They showed him around the galaxy and taught him all about their way of life, and Tommy was thrilled to be a part of it all.

As the years went by, Tommy continued to sneak out of his house at night to visit his alien friends. No one on Earth knew about his trips to space, and he kept his adventures a secret, never letting anyone in on the incredible journey he was taking.

But as he grew older, Tommy lost touch with his alien friends, and he always wondered what had happened to them. He hoped that one day, he would be able to see them again, and to continue exploring the mysteries of the universe.

Not Just a Mans Best Friend

When an alien named Jeratok first landed on Earth, he had no idea what to expect. He had always been alone in the vastness of space, and he had never encountered another living being before.

But as he wandered through the strange and unfamiliar landscape, he came across a little dog who was lost and alone. The dog was scared and hungry, and the alien could tell that he needed help.

Without hesitation, the alien picked up the dog and carried him back to his spacecraft. He knew that he had to do something to help the little creature, and he was determined to do everything he could to make him feel safe and secure.

As the days went by, the alien and the dog became inseparable. They spent hours playing together and exploring the universe, and they quickly became the best of friends.

The dog was fascinated by the alien's otherworldly powers, and he loved to watch him fly through the air and control the elements. And the alien was thrilled to have someone to share his adventures with, someone who was always there to cheer him on and make him laugh.

As the years went by, Jeratok and the dog continued to travel the cosmos, always together and always exploring. And they knew that no matter where they went, they would always be there for each other, through thick and thin.

My Bedroom Visitors

I was terrified when the aliens first appeared in my bedroom. They were tall and slender, with shimmering skin and glowing eyes, and they seemed to be studying me intently.

I tried to run, but it was no use - they were too fast, and before I knew it, I was being lifted off the ground and carried away. I screamed and struggled, but it was no use - I was completely at their mercy.

As we flew through the air, I could feel the cold wind whipping through my hair, and I knew that I was in deep trouble. I had no idea where the aliens were taking me, or what they had in store for me.

When we finally reached their spaceship, I was thrown into a sterile room and strapped to a table. The aliens began to poke and prod at me, examining every inch of my body with cold, clinical detachment.

I was terrified and humiliated, and I begged them to stop. But they ignored my pleas and continued their inspection, seemingly indifferent to my suffering.

As the hours ticked by, I knew that I had to find a way to escape. I had to get back to Earth, no matter what it took.

So I mustered all of my strength and courage, and I fought back. I kicked and thrashed and screamed, and I refused to give up.

And finally, after what felt like an eternity, the aliens relented. They released me from the table, and I stumbled out of the spaceship, dazed and confused but grateful to be alive.

I knew that I would never forget my alien abduction, and I vowed that I would never let it happen again. But as I looked up at the stars, I couldn't help but wonder what other mysteries the universe held in store for me.

The Extra-Terrestrial Affair

Donna and Erik had been together for years, and they had always been happy. They loved each other deeply, and they were excited to start a family together.

But when an alien named Zara appeared on the scene, everything changed. Zara was unlike anyone they had ever met - she was tall and slender, with shimmering skin and glowing eyes, and she seemed to have a special connection to Erik.

Zara told Erik that she had chosen him to be the father of her child. She explained that she had been searching for the perfect mate, and she believed that Erik was the one.

Erik was shocked and confused. He loved Donna and didn't want to hurt her, but he couldn't deny his attraction to Zara. He felt torn between the two women, and he didn't know what to do.

As if things weren't complicated enough, Donna revealed that she was pregnant too. She and Erik had been trying for a baby for a long time, and she was overjoyed to be expecting.

The three of them were in a difficult situation. They all wanted to be together, but they didn't know how to make it work. They argued and fought, each trying to persuade the others to see things their way.

But in the end, they came to a compromise. They decided to cohabitate and raise their children together, as one big, happy family.

And it worked - somehow, they managed to make it work. The alien baby and the human baby grew up in a loving home, surrounded by the love and support of their three parents. No one outside of their little family knew the truth, and they were happy to keep it that way.

As the years went by, the three of them grew closer and closer. They learned to love and accept each other, and they knew that they had found something special and rare. They were grateful to have each other, and they knew that they would always be there for each other, no matter what.

A Friendship to Never Forget

It was a typical summer day when the three teenagers - Sarah, Jack, and Dave - decided to go on a space exploration adventure. They had always been fascinated by the mysteries of the universe, and they were determined to see what was out there for themselves.

The trio set off in their homemade spacecraft, a rickety old contraption that they had built in their garage. It wasn't the most reliable vessel, but they were confident that it would get them where they needed to go.

As they flew through the vast expanse of space, they marveled at the wonders they saw. They passed through glowing nebulae and swirling galaxies, and they couldn't believe their luck at being able to witness such incredible sights.

But as they flew deeper into the unknown, they began to sense that something wasn't quite right. They couldn't quite put their finger on it, but they felt as if they were being watched.

And then, without warning, they were surrounded by a group of aliens. The aliens were tall and slender, with shimmering skin and glowing eyes, and they seemed to be studying the teenagers intently.

The teenagers were terrified, but they knew that they had to keep their cool if they wanted to make it out of this situation alive. So they tried to communicate with the aliens, hoping that they might be able to understand them.

To their surprise, the aliens responded, and they began to exchange ideas and information. The teenagers learned all about the aliens' way of life, and they were fascinated by the things they had to share.

But as the days went by, the teenagers began to realize that they might not be able to go home. They were thousands of lightyears from Earth, and they had no way of getting back.

Still, they refused to give up hope. They knew that they had to find a way to get home, no matter what it took. And they were determined to do whatever they could to make it happen...

The Alien Invasion

I was in the Oval Office when it happened. I was the President of the United States, and I was in the middle of an important meeting when the alarms went off.

I knew immediately that something was wrong. I could feel it in my gut - a sense of unease that I had never felt before.

I rushed to the window, and that's when I saw them. The aliens were everywhere - tall, slender creatures with shimmering skin and glowing eyes. They were swarming the White House, and they seemed to be everywhere at once.

I knew that I had to act fast. I grabbed the phone and called the military, ordering them to mobilize and defend the capital. I knew that this was going to be a fight to the death, and I was prepared to do whatever it took to win.

The battle raged on for hours. The aliens were fierce and relentless, and they seemed to be everywhere at once. But we were determined to hold our ground, and we fought back with everything we had.

As the sun began to rise, the aliens finally retreated. They had been beaten, and they knew that they couldn't win. They vanished into the morning sky, leaving behind a trail of destruction in their wake.

I stood on the White House lawn, surveying the damage. The building was in ruins, and there were bodies everywhere. It had been a brutal fight, but we had won.

I knew that this was just the beginning. The aliens would be back, and we would have to be ready. But for now, we had won, and we were safe.

I turned and walked back into the White House, ready to begin the long process of rebuilding and healing. We had survived the alien invasion, and we would emerge stronger than ever before.

A Pup's Best Friend

It was a typical day at the dog park when Max the golden retriever first met Koda. Koda was an unusual looking creature, with shimmering blue fur and glowing green eyes. He was smaller than Max, but he had an air of confidence about him that Max couldn't help but admire.

Koda told Max that he was an alien animal from a planet called Narubo. He had been brought to Earth by his master, a scientist who was studying the inhabitants of the planet. But when Koda's master left him behind, he had no choice but to find a new home.

Max was fascinated by Koda's story, and he immediately offered to help him find a new home. He knew that Koda was a good creature, and he didn't want to see him stuck on Earth all alone.

So the two of them set off on a journey, determined to find a new home for Koda. They traveled far and wide, encountering all sorts of strange and wonderful creatures along the way.

As they journeyed, Max and Koda became the best of friends. They learned to rely on each other and support one another, and they knew that they could always count on each other no matter what.

Finally, after many long months, they found a new home for Koda. It was a wonderful place, filled with humans who loved and cared for him. And Max knew that Koda would be happy there, surrounded by people who cared about him.

As Max said goodbye to his alien friend, he knew that he would never forget the journey they had shared. And he knew that Koda would always be a special part of his life, no matter where they were or what they were doing.

The House That Haunts Them

The Adamms family had just moved into their new home, a charming two-story house nestled beside an old graveyard. Unbeknownst to them, the house had once served as a mortuary, a place where the deceased were prepared for their final rest.

Excitement turned to unease as strange occurrences began to unfold. Doors creaked open on their own accord, and chilling drafts swept through rooms, carrying whispers from the forgotten past. The family tried to dismiss these incidents as mere quirks of an old house, but the truth was far more unsettling.

Late one stormy night, as the rain pelted the roof and lightning illuminated the darkened graveyard, the Adamms family found themselves inexplicably drawn to the attic. There, hidden beneath dusty sheets, they discovered a worn journal—a relic of the mortuary's former caretaker.

The journal spoke of a dark secret that lay entwined with the very foundation of the house. The deceased buried in the adjacent graveyard had once been close friends of the caretaker, who, upon their passing, could not bear to part with them. Instead, he brought their remains into the mortuary, where he meticulously attended to their every need, even in death.

As the family continued to read the journal, a haunting presence crept into their lives. Apparitions of the deceased materialized in the halls, their ethereal figures a stark reminder of the mortuary's twisted past. The spirits longed for release, yearning to find peace in the afterlife, but their connection to the house held them captive.

Tormented by their presence, the Adamms family delved deeper into the house's history. They sought guidance from spiritualists and paranormal experts, desperate to uncover a way to break the spirits' bonds. Together, they unearthed a forgotten ritual, a last hope for the restless souls and the living alike.

Gathering in the heart of the graveyard, beneath a moonlit sky, the family performed the ritual. They chanted ancient incantations and offered heartfelt prayers, beseeching the spirits to let go of the mortal realm and find solace in the beyond. A solemn silence settled over the graveyard as the spirits, one by one, embraced the light and ascended towards eternal peace.

With the spirits finally released, the house beside the graveyard became still, no longer haunted by the echoes of the past. The Adamms family, forever changed by their encounter, found solace in knowing they had helped the departed find their rightful place in the universe.

And so, the house by the graveyard, once a mortuary entwined with sorrow and restless souls, stood as a testament to the power of compassion and the redemptive nature of closure.

The Forgotten Melody

In the small, picturesque town of Willowbrook, a dilapidated Victorian mansion stood abandoned at the edge of the woods. Legend had it that the house was haunted by the ghost of a renowned pianist named Amelia Sinclair.

Amelia had been a prodigious talent, her fingers gliding effortlessly across the keys, enchanting all who heard her melodies. But one fateful night, as she performed her masterpiece in the grand hall of her mansion, tragedy struck. The audience was captivated by her music when suddenly, in the midst of a crescendo, Amelia's heart gave out, and she collapsed onto the piano, her final notes fading into silence.

Years later, the neglected mansion became the talk of the town once again when a young pianist named Emily arrived. Drawn by the allure of the forgotten house and its rumored haunting, she sought inspiration for her own music within its decaying walls.

One moonlit night, Emily cautiously approached the mansion's weathered doors. As she stepped inside, a soft, melancholic melody filled the air, the notes floating delicately from the grand piano in the corner. Curiosity consumed her, and she couldn't resist sitting at the piano bench.

Her fingers trembled as they touched the keys, and to her amazement, the music flowed effortlessly. It was as if Amelia herself guided her hands, her spirit longing to share her unfinished symphony with the world.

Night after night, Emily returned to the mansion, playing the forgotten melody that Amelia had left behind. The haunting strains echoed through the hallways, captivating not only the living but also the ethereal presence of Amelia.

Word of Emily's remarkable performances spread, drawing crowds from far and wide to witness the ghostly collaboration. The mansion, once an empty shell, now pulsed with the vibrancy of music and the energy of two souls united through time.

But as Emily grew more deeply entwined with the spirit of Amelia, she noticed a subtle change. The once serene atmosphere of the mansion turned ominous, and the music took on an eerie, dissonant quality. It became clear that Amelia's spirit was growing restless, longing to be set free.

(Continued...)

In a desperate bid to release Amelia from her eternal plight, Emily embarked on a journey to uncover the truth behind the unfinished melody. She delved into dusty archives and spoke with elders of the town, unearthing a long-lost chapter of Amelia's life.

Determined to honor Amelia's memory, Emily composed the final movements of the symphony, infusing it with her own soulful touch. As she played the closing notes, a shimmering figure materialized beside her—the spirit of Amelia herself.

Amelia's eyes brimmed with gratitude as her ghostly form dissipated, leaving behind a sense of peace that enveloped the mansion. Emily had given her the closure she had longed for, setting her spirit free to join the eternal chorus of the great beyond.

From that day forward, the forgotten mansion of Willowbrook stood as a testament to the power of music, and the enduring bond between two musicians—Emily and Amelia—whose harmonies transcended time itself.

The Unseen Intrusion

I never believed in the supernatural until that fateful night when an unexplained energy took hold of me, invading my very being.

It started innocently enough. I was visiting an antique shop, searching for a unique piece to add to my collection. My eyes were drawn to an old, weathered necklace adorned with an intricately carved pendant. As I placed it around my neck, a strange sensation washed over me, like a shiver that crawled down my spine.

That night, as I lay in bed, an eerie stillness enveloped the room. I felt an unyielding presence lurking in the darkness, unseen but unmistakable. Suddenly, an invisible force gripped my body, rendering me motionless. Panic surged through me as I realized I was no longer in control.

The energy coursed through my veins, its foreign power overwhelming and invasive. I watched, a mere spectator within my own body, as my limbs moved of their own accord. I tried to scream, to fight back against the unseen intruder, but my voice was silenced, held captive by this mysterious force.

Days turned into weeks, and the episodes persisted. The energy toyed with my emotions, manipulating my thoughts and actions. I became a vessel for its desires, carrying out tasks that were not my own, alien to my very nature. Friends and family noticed the change, expressing concern for the person I had become.

Determined to reclaim my autonomy, I sought answers in the depths of research and the counsel of experts. They spoke of ancient legends and tales of possession, warning me of the dangers that awaited if I did not sever the connection with the enigmatic energy that held me captive.

Guided by their wisdom, I embarked on a perilous journey to uncover the truth. I sought out spiritual healers and performed cleansing rituals, hoping to banish the entity that had taken root within me. Each attempt brought fleeting moments of liberation, but the force proved resilient, always returning with renewed vigor.

It was during a solitary retreat to a remote, sacred place that I encountered an aged seer—a wise soul who had spent a lifetime studying the intricacies of the spiritual realm. With a gentle touch, the seer revealed the source of my torment: a long-lost spirit trapped between realms, seeking solace through a human vessel.

Together, we delved deep into meditation, forging a connection with the wandering spirit. Through whispered prayers and empathetic understanding, we offered the lost soul a pathway to liberation, a chance to find peace and resolution.

In a moment of transcendence, the energy that had gripped me began to dissipate, gradually releasing its hold. As the veil of possession lifted, I could finally breathe freely, feeling the warmth of my own soul return.

The experience forever changed me, reminding me of the mysterious forces that dwell beyond our realm of understanding. I carry the memory of that intrusion, a reminder to cherish the autonomy we often take for granted. And though the energy has departed, I remain forever wary, knowing that the line between the seen and the unseen is thinner than we can ever comprehend.

The Cursed Stone

In the quiet town of Ravenswood, an ancient stone lay forgotten beneath the abandoned graveyard. Unbeknownst to the townsfolk, the stone held a malevolent curse, a relic of a dark past. When the time came for a new subdivision to be developed, the workers unknowingly unearthed the stone while preparing the land for the second phase of homes.

Among the laborers was Jack, an ordinary man with an extraordinary affinity for energy. Drawn to the stone's mysterious aura, he picked it up without hesitation. Little did he know, his fateful decision transferred the curse onto him.

As the days passed, Jack's world began to crumble. Shadows danced before his eyes, ominous and malicious. Demonic figures haunted his dreams, tormenting his waking hours. An unexplained illness plagued his body, weakening him from within. Desperate for answers, he sought help from countless doctors, but they could find no cause for his suffering.

Haunted by his worsening condition, Jack retraced his steps, searching for a connection to his misery. It was then he realized the truth: the stone he had found, now hidden away in a safe within his house, was the source of his torment.

Driven by a newfound determination, Jack attempted to rid himself of the cursed stone. He hurled it into the depths of a river, hoping it would be carried away by the current. But the stone resurfaced, as if taunting him with its unyielding presence.

Undeterred, Jack tried to destroy it by driving over it with his car, but the stone remained unscathed, mocking his efforts. In a last-ditch attempt, he discarded it in a trash bin, only to find it back in his possession the next morning, as if it had never left.

(Continued...)

Feeling trapped and terrified, Jack locked the stone away in the safe once more, hoping to find a way to break its grip. But fate had other plans. One night, a daring thief broke into Jack's house, drawn by rumors of the valuable contents within the safe. Unaware of the stone's curse, the thief cracked it open, and his fingers brushed against the ancient artifact.

In an instant, the curse transferred to the thief, freeing Jack from its clutches. The thief's mind cleared, his soul liberated from the malevolent presence. Overwhelmed by the experience, he vowed to never touch another stone again, forever changed by the ordeal.

As for the cursed stone, its fate remained unknown. It vanished into the depths of history, its dark energy extinguished, leaving behind a cautionary tale and a reminder of the ancient forces that can still lay dormant, waiting to ensnare the unsuspecting.

And so, Ravenswood stood as a testament to the power of curses and the fragility of the human spirit, reminding all who dared to listen that some stones are better left undisturbed, their secrets forever buried within the earth.

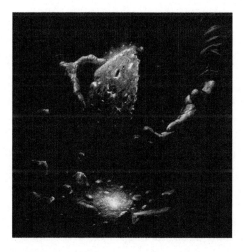

The Far Out Journey

In the quiet slumber of his bedroom, young Timmy fell into a deep sleep. In his dream, his father appeared, holding a shimmering pass in his hands. "This is a special ticket," his dad said with a smile. "It can make you anything you want to be."

Timmy's heart fluttered with excitement. "I want to be an alien," he declared. "I don't like school or the people there. They make me feel like I'm from another planet."

With a wave of his hand, his dad activated the ticket, enveloping Timmy in a bright light. In an instant, he transformed into an extraterrestrial being, complete with green skin, large eyes, and incredible superpowers.

With his newfound abilities, Timmy soared into the night sky. He raced against time to stop a massive meteor hurtling towards Earth. The planet's fate hung in the balance as he summoned his powers to deflect the cosmic threat.

Despite his valiant efforts, the impact of the meteor overwhelmed Timmy's alien form. He vanished into stardust, sacrificing himself to save the world.

News of Timmy's heroic act spread like wildfire, and the people hailed him as a true champion. They celebrated his selflessness, remembering him as the little boy who became an alien to protect them all.

Timmy's sacrifice left an indelible mark on the hearts of those he saved. His legacy lived on, reminding everyone that true heroes come in all forms, even those who may feel like aliens in a world that doesn't understand them.

And though his time as an alien was short-lived, Timmy's spirit forever remained an inspiration, reminding us all that the power to make a difference lies within us, no matter who we are or where we come from.

A Spectral Feline

In a quaint little town, a peculiar cat named Whiskers possessed a unique gift. Whiskers had the uncanny ability to see ghosts that roamed the earthly realm. These playful apparitions, with their mischievous tendencies, turned Whiskers' life into a hilarious adventure.

As soon as Whiskers moved into a creaky old house, the ghosts revealed themselves, pulling whimsical pranks on one another. Objects floated through the air, cushions were rearranged, and invisible hands tickled unsuspecting specters. Whiskers watched with wide-eyed amusement, purring with delight at the sight of these spectral antics.

The ghosts quickly realized that Whiskers could see them. They danced around the cat, tugging at its tail and swatting playfully. Whiskers embraced their company, leaping and pouncing as if engaged in an invisible game of tag.

Together, Whiskers and the ghosts formed an unusual but endearing family. They shared meals, with ghostly hands pretending to hold invisible forks, and engaged in spirited conversations that only Whiskers could comprehend.

The house was filled with laughter as the ghosts enacted elaborate pranks on one another. Sheets were pulled over their heads, and they floated through walls, pretending to be phantoms in a haunted play. Whiskers chased after their transparent forms, joining in on the comedic frolics.

As time went on, the bond between Whiskers and the ghosts deepened. The specters, once lonely souls, found solace in Whiskers' companionship, and the cat reveled in the joyous energy that surrounded them.

Neighborhood children would often visit, captivated by the house's reputation for ghostly encounters. Whiskers became the star of their stories, regaling them with tales of the funny pranks the ghosts played on one another. The children laughed and giggled, their imaginations ignited by Whiskers' enchanting tales.

Days turned into months, and months into years, as the comedic pranks and playful camaraderie continued. Whiskers basked in the love and warmth of its spectral family, its life forever intertwined with theirs.

And so, in that quaint little house, where spirits roamed and laughter filled the air, Whiskers and the ghosts found solace and belonging. Their bond transcended the realms of the living and the dead, proving that even in the most unusual of circumstances, friendship can bloom and laughter can heal even the most ethereal hearts.

The Whispering Woods

Deep within the heart of Whispering Woods, an ancient forest shrouded in mystery, something inexplicable was happening. It started with a faint hum—a subtle vibration felt by those who ventured too close. Curiosity drew them deeper, unable to resist the allure of the unknown.

As word spread, a small group of intrepid explorers gathered at the forest's edge, their hearts pounding with anticipation. Armed with cameras, recorders, and their own determination, they stepped into the enigmatic realm of Whispering Woods.

The air grew thick as they ventured further, a hushed silence blanketing the trees. The forest seemed alive, whispering secrets that eluded comprehension. Shadows danced amidst the foliage, playing tricks on the eyes of the wary travelers.

Suddenly, a powerful gust of wind tore through the woods, bending trees and rustling leaves with a force that defied explanation. An eerie chill gripped the air, as if the forest itself had come alive.

The explorers pressed on, their curiosity outweighing their apprehension. That's when they stumbled upon it—a hidden clearing, bathed in ethereal light. In the center stood a circle of ancient stones, their origins lost to time. Intricate symbols adorned their weathered surfaces, pulsating with an otherworldly energy.

Captivated by the sight, the explorers drew closer, their hands outstretched to touch the stones. But before their fingers made contact, a blinding flash enveloped the clearing, and the ground trembled beneath their feet...

(Continued...)

When the light dissipated, the explorers found themselves scattered throughout the forest, disoriented and alone. Panic set in as they called out to one another, their voices swallowed by the dense foliage.

As night fell, the forest awakened with strange sounds—a symphony of whispers that seemed to echo from every direction. The explorers stumbled through the darkened woods, their hearts pounding with fear. Something inexplicable was happening, but the answers remained just beyond their grasp.

Exhausted and overwhelmed, the explorers regrouped at the clearing, their minds racing with theories and questions. What force resided within Whispering Woods? What had become of their companions? And, most importantly, how could they escape this living nightmare?

With a renewed sense of determination, they vowed to unravel the forest's secrets and find their missing comrades. They would face the unexplained phenomenon head-on, for their survival and the truth that lay hidden within Whispering Woods.

But as the explorers ventured deeper into the mysterious forest, an ominous presence watched from the shadows. Its true nature, and the fate of the trapped souls, remained concealed, leaving the readers on the edge of their seat, craving answers to the enigma of Whispering Woods.

The Silent Reflection

In the quiet town of Stillwater, a strange occurrence seized the community. Every night, at precisely 11:11 p.m., a mirror in the town's old Victorian mansion emitted an eerie glow. The residents were both fascinated and unsettled by the unexplained phenomenon.

Curiosity got the best of me, and one night I decided to investigate. As the clock struck 11:11, I cautiously approached the mansion, heart pounding in my chest. The glow intensified as I reached the mirror, its surface pulsating with an otherworldly energy.

Reflected within the glass was a shadowy figure, indiscernible yet undeniably present. Its form seemed to shift and contort, defying logic and stirring primal fear within me.

Unable to tear my gaze away, I watched in horror as the figure reached out from the mirror, its hand extending beyond the boundary of glass. Frozen in disbelief, I felt an icy chill crawl up my spine as the figure's finger brushed against my own reflection.

A surge of inexplicable sensations overcame me. Whispers echoed through my mind, foreign and haunting. Visions flashed before my eyes, fragments of a forgotten past. The figure seemed to be imparting a message, but its meaning remained elusive.

Days turned into weeks, and the mysterious encounters persisted. I delved into research, seeking answers to the enigma that had consumed me. But the more I unearthed, the deeper the mystery became. There was no record of the mirror's origin or the shadowy figure it summoned.

Night after night, I found myself drawn back to the mansion, unable to resist the call of the unknown. Each time, the figure seemed to grow more agitated, its presence more tangible.

As I ventured closer to unveiling the truth, a foreboding sensation crept over me. I realized that the mirror and the figure were intertwined, their existence dependent on each other. The figure sought release, but at what cost?

In a moment of desperate decision, I summoned the courage to shatter the mirror, hoping to free the figure from its ethereal prison. Yet, as the glass splintered and shattered, the figure's silhouette vanished, leaving behind a chilling silence that hung in the air.

Though the figure was gone, the lingering question remained: What had I unleashed? The reflection had been broken, but the true nature of the phenomenon remained obscured, leaving me on the precipice of discovery, yearning to uncover the untold secrets that lurked within the shattered fragments.

Elusive Companions

In a quaint neighborhood, young Sam found himself inexplicably drawn to a dog he would often spot wandering the streets. Its fur was a rich, golden hue, and its eyes radiated a gentle warmth. Sam was captivated by the dog's presence, feeling an unspoken connection that tugged at his heart.

Day after day, Sam eagerly called out to the dog, hoping to forge a bond. But no matter how hard he tried, the dog would only watch from a distance, as if keeping a mysterious secret. Undeterred, Sam persisted, leaving treats and kind words in the hope of gaining its trust.

Weeks turned into months, and the elusive dog began to reveal glimmers of interest. It cautiously approached Sam, sniffing his outstretched hand, yet always retreating before any physical contact could be made. Sam refused to give up, understanding that earning the dog's trust would require patience and understanding.

Finally, the day came when the dog allowed Sam to approach. It wagged its tail tentatively, as if unsure of its decision. Excitement and joy surged through Sam's veins, and he knew he had reached a turning point.

Carefully, Sam led the dog home, envisioning the joy on his parents' faces as they welcomed their new furry companion. But when he burst through the front door, filled with boundless enthusiasm, his parents' expressions were filled with confusion and concern.

"Mom, Dad, look! I've finally convinced the dog to come home with me!" Sam exclaimed, pointing to his newfound friend.

To Sam's dismay, his parents gazed into an empty space. Their eyes, once filled with love and warmth, were now clouded with bewilderment. It was as if the dog was invisible to them, an apparition that only Sam could see and feel.

Tears welled up in Sam's eyes as he struggled to understand. How could his parents not see the dog that had become such a significant part of his life? Confusion enveloped him, and a sense of isolation settled in his heart.

In the days that followed, Sam continued to interact with the dog, cherishing their unspoken bond. Together, they explored the world, finding solace in each other's presence. Sam shared his secrets, dreams, and fears, knowing that the dog listened intently, even if no one else could see it.

As the years went by, the invisible dog became Sam's steadfast companion, an ethereal guardian that guided him through life's challenges. Although the world couldn't comprehend the bond they shared, Sam embraced the mystery and the unexplainable, finding comfort in the inexplicable connection that defied the boundaries of reality.

And so, the invisible dog remained a silent enigma, forever entwined with Sam's existence. Their extraordinary companionship, witnessed only by the boy himself, would forever serve as a reminder that sometimes, the most profound connections cannot be seen or understood, yet their impact on our lives is immeasurable.

The Tale of Slender Man

In the depths of the shadowy forest, a legend whispered among those brave enough to share it—the tale of the Slender Man. Tall and faceless, draped in a suit that seemed to merge with the darkness, the Slender Man instilled fear in the hearts of those who dared to speak its name.

The story went that the Slender Man lurked within the woods, its elongated limbs reaching out like tendrils, ensnaring the unsuspecting. It was said that once one caught a glimpse of its form, an eerie sensation would settle in—a feeling of being watched, even in the safety of daylight.

Among the many stories told, one stood out—a tale of a young girl named Emily who became entangled in the web of the Slender Man's sinister presence. Emily, an inquisitive soul, had always been drawn to the mysteries that lingered at the fringes of reality.

One fateful evening, while exploring the outskirts of the forest, Emily glimpsed a figure in the distance—a tall, faceless silhouette that seemed to sway and flicker. Fear mingled with curiosity as she cautiously approached, unable to resist the lure of the unknown.

As Emily delved deeper into the heart of the forest, the atmosphere grew heavy with a foreboding energy. Shadows danced amidst the trees, playing tricks on her eyes. Strange symbols materialized on the trunks, as if etched by an invisible hand.

The whispers of the Slender Man echoed through the night, chilling Emily's very core. It watched her every move, its presence a haunting reminder that she had trespassed into its realm.

Weeks turned into months, and Emily found herself consumed by the Slender Man's influence. She began to see it in her dreams, its featureless face haunting her every sleeping hour. The boundaries between reality and nightmare blurred, as if the Slender Man had taken residence within her mind.

Terrified, Emily sought refuge in the solace of daylight, but even there, the Slender Man's presence lingered. It seemed to lurk in every corner, in every reflection, an ever-present reminder of the darkness that clung to her.

(Continued...)

Determined to break free from the Slender Man's grasp, Emily embarked on a quest for answers. She delved into ancient texts and sought the counsel of wise sages who spoke of rituals and incantations. The path was treacherous, but Emily's determination burned bright.

With each step, she unraveled the mysteries of the Slender Man. She discovered that the entity fed on fear and despair, growing stronger with each trembling heart it claimed. Armed with newfound knowledge, Emily resolved to confront her fears head-on.

In a climactic encounter, Emily faced the Slender Man, its form towering before her. She summoned courage from the depths of her being, refusing to succumb to its influence any longer. With a defiant spirit, she uttered words of power, banishing the Slender Man back into the shadows from whence it came.

As the Slender Man faded away, Emily emerged from the ordeal forever changed. The scars of her encounter remained, a reminder of the darkness that exists in the world. But she carried with her a newfound strength, a resilience born from her battle with the unknown.

The tale of Emily and the Slender Man became a legend itself, cautioning those who would tread the path of curiosity and reminding them of the dangers that await in the realm of the supernatural. The forest stood as a silent witness, the haunting echoes of the Slender Man's presence serving as a chilling reminder that some legends are best left undisturbed.

The Haunting Inheritance

The Thompson family had inherited a grand old house, a gift from their late great-uncle whom they had never met. Excitement filled the air as they moved into their new abode, unaware of the dark secrets that lay dormant within its walls.

Soon after settling in, the family's peaceful nights turned into harrowing nightmares. Strange occurrences plagued their sleep. They felt an invisible force lifting them from their beds, hurling them across the room, and leaving painful scratches upon their flesh. The spirits within the house seemed determined to torment them.

Frightened and desperate for respite, the Thompsons sought solace in the rituals of their faith. They invited a pastor to bless the house, hoping to ward off the malevolent presence. But even the holy man was not immune to the wrath of the entity. As he attempted to perform the ritual, he was attacked, his body assaulted by unseen forces.

The family's hope wavered, their nerves frayed. The final straw came when the mother, Sarah, was dragged towards the well on the property, her terrified screams piercing the night. In a race against time, her husband, John, awakened from a deep sleep, mustered his strength, and rushed to her aid. With a last surge of energy, Sarah fought her way back to safety, just inches from being pulled into the abyss.

Shaken to the core, the Thompsons knew they could no longer endure the relentless torment. They made a decision in the dead of night to flee the cursed home, leaving their belongings behind as an offering to the malevolent spirits.

As they sped away from the house, the weight of their ordeal slowly lifted. Yet, their memories remained haunted by the darkness they had faced. The spirits had claimed their home, but the Thompsons were determined to rebuild their lives, free from the clutches of the supernatural.

Years passed, and whispers of the abandoned house continued to circulate. Tales of its restless spirits became the stuff of local legends, a cautionary tale of the unseen forces that lurked within. And as the Thompsons rebuilt their lives in a new home, they carried the scars of their encounter, forever aware of the thin veil that separates the living from the realm of the spirits.

The house stood as a silent testament to the inexplicable, its abandoned halls a constant reminder of the family's harrowing escape. And while the Thompsons had left behind their belongings, they could never truly leave behind the memories of the demons that had lurked in the darkness, waiting to claim them as their own.

The Curse of the Painted Lady

In the heart of a medieval village, nestled amidst towering castles and cobblestone streets, a group of six talented artists set out on a remarkable collaboration. Drawn together by their shared passion for creativity, they embarked on a project that would forever alter their lives—the creation of a painting that would come to be known as "The Enigmatic Portrait."

With meticulous care and unwavering dedication, the artists poured their souls into the masterpiece, each stroke capturing the essence of the enigmatic woman at its center. But as the final brushstrokes were applied, a sense of unease settled upon them. The woman they had painted seemed to come alive, her haunting beauty radiating from the canvas.

Soon after the completion of their masterpiece, the artists began to experience vivid and unsettling dreams. In their slumber, the woman from the painting appeared before them, her ethereal presence filling their minds with enchanting whispers and unsettling visions.

Night after night, the dreams grew darker and more foreboding. The artists became lost within the labyrinth of their own creations, tormented by the specter that haunted their every sleeping hour. The woman's alluring gaze turned into a malevolent glare, and her voice transformed into an eerie symphony of madness.

As the days passed, a chilling pattern emerged. One by one, the artists met their demise, each falling victim to a fate as macabre as the paintings they had created. Some were driven to madness, their souls consumed by an insatiable darkness. Others met untimely accidents, their lives cut short by inexplicable circumstances.

The villagers whispered of a curse—a curse that had been summoned forth from the depths of the artists' collective imagination. They spoke of the woman from the painting, her vengeful spirit exacting retribution upon those who dared to immortalize her image.

(Continued...)

In their final moments, the artists came to realize the true nature of their creation. They had unwittingly breathed life into a malevolent force, one that sought to claim their souls as payment for the art they had crafted.

As the last artist succumbed to the relentless torment, the village shuddered with a mixture of sorrow and relief. The Enigmatic Portrait was hidden away, a somber reminder of the tragedy that had unfolded within its brushstrokes.

To this day, the painting remains locked in the depths of the village's archives, its haunting presence serving as a cautionary tale to those who dare to delve into the realm of creativity. The artists' collective creation became a testament to the fine line that exists between artistic mastery and the dark forces that lie hidden within the human imagination.

And as the years pass, the villagers continue to recount the tale, their voices laced with a mix of awe and trepidation. They speak of the artists who fell victim to their own creation, a reminder that some art, no matter how beautiful, can unleash a power beyond comprehension—an enigmatic force that demands a heavy price.

The Clown of a Cursed Town

In the town of Ravensbridge, the legend of the Cursed Clown whispered through the autumn winds. Benjamin Bloom, once a beloved clown, met a tragic end that stained the spirit of Halloween.

On each Halloween night, Benjamin's ghost rose from the earth, clad in tattered clown attire. He roamed the streets, seeking solace in the chilling air. Parents warned their children not to venture out, for the specter of the Cursed Clown awaited those who strayed.

Curiosity overcame fear, and some children defied the warnings. The cursed clown lurked in the shadows, luring them closer with an ethereal presence. Those who encountered him found themselves ensnared in his grasp, their fates sealed as the moon reached its zenith.

Ravensbridge mourned the lost children, forever marked by the cursed clown's malevolence. Halloween became a somber occasion, a night of remembrance for innocent souls taken by the vengeful spirit.

To this day, the legend of the Cursed Clown haunts Ravensbridge, a chilling reminder of the darkness that can consume a once joyful heart. Residents keep watch, hoping to protect the children from the tragic fate that awaits those who dare cross paths with Benjamin Bloom—the Cursed Clown.

'Another Realm App'

In the bustling city of Arcadia, a young boy named Max stumbled upon a mysterious cell phone app called "Another Realm." Intrigued, he downloaded it, expecting an exciting new game to fill his days with adventure. Little did he know, his curiosity would lead him to a perilous journey beyond his wildest imagination.

As Max tapped on the app icon, his surroundings began to distort. In an instant, he found himself transported to a realm far removed from his own—a world teeming with spirits, demons, and warlocks. Panic gripped his heart as he realized he had been sucked into the very game he thought was mere entertainment.

Max searched frantically for a way back home, but the game's mechanics were unlike anything he had ever encountered. It was a treacherous landscape, filled with labyrinthine forests, foreboding castles, and ethereal realms. Each step he took was fraught with danger, as supernatural creatures lurked in every shadow.

Haunted by the spirits of the realm, Max discovered that not all of them were malevolent. Some sought to help him find a way back to his world, offering cryptic clues and guidance. Others, however, delighted in his predicament, taunting him with riddles and tricks, their intentions shrouded in mystery.

Max's only hope lay in unraveling the secrets of the realm and finding a way to overcome the challenges that awaited him. He met an ancient warlock who possessed knowledge of the game's dark magic, offering guidance in exchange for Max's loyalty. Reluctantly, Max formed an uneasy alliance, realizing that he needed the warlock's expertise to navigate the treacherous terrain.

Together, they embarked on a perilous quest, battling demons and deciphering cryptic symbols etched into ancient stones. Max's bravery was tested at every turn as he confronted his deepest fears and faced the formidable warlocks who held the keys to his escape.

(Continued...)

As days turned into weeks, Max's determination grew unwavering.
The spirits, demons, and warlocks gradually revealed fragments of
the realm's history and its connection to his own world. It became
clear that Max's presence in the realm was no accident—that he held
a pivotal role in the balance between the two worlds.

With newfound allies and hard-won knowledge, Max devised a plan
to challenge the game's powerful creator, a reclusive deity who
thrived on the suffering of trapped souls. In a climactic showdown,
Max confronted the deity, armed with his unwavering courage and
the support of the spirits who believed in him.

Through wit and sheer will, Max outsmarted the creator, breaking the
barrier that held him captive. The realm trembled as Max returned to
Arcadia, his heart brimming with lessons learned and newfound
strength. He would forever carry the memories of his extraordinary
journey, a testament to the resilience of the human spirit in the face
of unimaginable odds.

And as Max closed the "Another Realm" app for the final time, he
knew that the realm would forever hold a place in his heart—a
testament to his indomitable spirit and the boundless potential of a
young boy who had ventured beyond the ordinary into a world of
spirits, demons, and warlocks, emerging triumphant against all odds.

Triumph Over the Malevolent Shadows

In the quiet suburban town of Crestwood, the Johnson family unknowingly became the target of a malevolent force—a poltergeist that sought to steal their innocence and disturb the peace within their home.

Strange occurrences began to plague the Johnsons, escalating from minor disturbances to unnerving events that disrupted their daily lives. Objects would inexplicably move, doors slammed shut without warning, and eerie whispers echoed through the halls when the house lay still.

The poltergeist reveled in the chaos it sowed, feeding off the fear and vulnerability of its victims. It played sinister games, preying upon the family's innocence, attempting to shatter their sense of security.

As the days turned into nights, the Johnsons' once-happy home transformed into a battleground, filled with unease and tension. The children, once carefree and playful, grew anxious and afraid. Shadows danced on their walls, and disembodied laughter echoed in their dreams.

The family sought solace in their shared struggles, uniting against the malevolent entity that haunted them. They enlisted the help of paranormal investigators and spiritual guides, desperate to reclaim their lives from the clutches of the poltergeist.

Together, they conducted rituals and cleansings, trying to rid their home of the sinister presence. But the poltergeist was relentless, its malevolence seeping into the very fabric of their existence. It seemed determined to tear apart their innocence and leave them forever scarred.

Yet, in the face of darkness, the Johnsons discovered an inner strength they never knew they possessed. They refused to let fear consume them, finding solace in their love and unwavering bond. They shielded their children from the malevolence, creating a sanctuary of love and protection amidst the chaos.

(Continued...)

Slowly, their resilience began to weaken the poltergeist's grip. With each act of defiance, the family reclaimed a piece of their innocence, refusing to succumb to the darkness that sought to engulf them.

In a final confrontation, the Johnsons stood united, facing the poltergeist with unwavering courage. They confronted their deepest fears head-on, unmasking the entity's desperate attempts to steal their innocence. Their love, fortified by their shared determination, proved to be a formidable force against the malevolence that had plagued them.

As the light of dawn broke, the poltergeist retreated, vanishing into the shadows from whence it came. The Johnsons emerged victorious, their innocence intact, their spirits indomitable. The house, once a battlefield, was restored to a haven of peace and tranquility.

The Johnsons' story became a testament to the resilience of the human spirit in the face of darkness. It served as a reminder that love, unity, and the unwavering belief in one's innocence can triumph over even the most malevolent forces.

And as the Johnson family moved forward, forever changed by their encounter, they embraced their newfound strength and cherished the innocence they had fought so fiercely to protect. Their story served as a beacon of hope to others who faced similar battles, inspiring them to stand tall in the face of darkness and reclaim their own innocence from the clutches of malevolence.

Writers Block Crazy

In the dusty attic of an old Victorian house, a haunted typewriter lay forgotten. Its keys sat still, stained with the ink of a tortured author's unfinished words.

Long ago, a once-promising writer sought solace in his craft. But as the weight of his own expectations grew unbearable, his words faded, and a suffocating writer's block consumed him. Desperate to find inspiration, he locked himself in the attic, vowing to write until his masterpiece emerged.

Days turned into weeks, and weeks into months. The author, secluded from the world, wrestled with his demons. But as hunger gnawed at his belly and sleep deprivation took hold, his mind became a chaotic labyrinth of half-formed sentences and shattered dreams.

In the darkness of that lonely room, the typewriter absorbed the author's anguish, becoming a vessel for his tortured soul. Its keys clacked and rattled, possessed by a phantom force. The typewriter yearned to bring forth the author's words, to release the bottled creativity that had driven him to madness.

Yet, the writer's resolve waned. He succumbed to the torment of his own mind, withering away into a mere specter of his former self. The typewriter, abandoned and cursed, bore witness to his tragic demise.

To this day, the haunted typewriter remains a testament to the destructive power of creative frustration. Its keys occasionally stir, a phantom echo of the author's failed aspirations. But the room remains locked, the words forever trapped within its walls—a chilling reminder of the price one may pay for artistic brilliance.

Imagine Train Express

In the small town of Willowbrook, an enigmatic phenomenon unfolded night after night—a train that materialized fleetingly, only to vanish into the depths of darkness. The townsfolk watched in awe as this spectral locomotive passed through, leaving behind nothing but a trail of ethereal smoke from its chimney.

No one could explain the train's origin or purpose. It appeared at the stroke of midnight, its haunting whistle echoing through the quiet streets. As the townspeople gathered, their breath caught in anticipation, knowing they had just a brief moment to witness this extraordinary spectacle.

The train emerged from the veil of night, its vintage carriages gleaming with an otherworldly glow. Its wheels clicked and clacked along the tracks, as if propelled by some mysterious force. Each detail was etched in the memories of those who witnessed its fleeting presence—a majestic locomotive, adorned with intricate engravings, and windows that reflected the moon's gentle light.

As the train passed through Willowbrook, a mesmerizing aura engulfed the town. The air crackled with an intangible energy, as if time itself held its breath. Some claimed to have glimpsed passengers within the carriages—ghostly figures from a bygone era, their expressions etched with both sorrow and longing.

But as quickly as it arrived, the train vanished, leaving nothing but the echo of its rumbling engine and the dissipating smoke from its chimney. The townspeople were left pondering its purpose—was it a vessel for lost souls, forever trapped in transit? Or did it serve as a fleeting portal to another realm, a glimpse into the mysteries that lay beyond?

(Continued...)

Speculation abounded, stories were woven, and the train became an integral part of Willowbrook's folklore. Children would gather by the tracks, dreaming of adventures beyond the mortal realm, while elders whispered tales of those who had boarded the train and returned forever changed.

The train's apparitions grew intertwined with the fabric of the town, a symbol of wonder and the transient nature of life itself. It served as a reminder that some phenomena eluded rational explanation, inviting the townspeople to embrace the mystical and find solace in the unknown.

Night after night, the train continued its spectral journey, passing through Willowbrook, illuminating the darkness with its ethereal presence. And though the townspeople could never truly grasp its secrets, they cherished the fleeting moments they shared with the enigmatic locomotive—the train that emerged from the shadows, leaving behind only whispers and the lingering scent of smoke as it disappeared into the night.

Golden Blossom Phenomenon

In the quaint town of Crestwood, a peculiar phenomenon cast its enchanting spell on the residents. Each year, on the eve of the summer solstice, the night sky illuminated with a mesmerizing display—a shower of shimmering golden petals gently cascading from above.

The townspeople gathered in awe as the golden petals descended, filling the air with an ethereal glow. The phenomenon, known as the "Golden Blossom Rain," had been an enigma for generations, defying scientific explanation and captivating the hearts of all who witnessed it.

As the golden petals gracefully fell, they carried with them a sense of wonder and joy. Children danced in the streets, reaching out to catch the elusive blossoms, their laughter blending with the ethereal melody that accompanied the phenomenon.

The Golden Blossom Rain became a cherished tradition, celebrated with a vibrant festival that united the community. Streets were adorned with shimmering decorations, and the townspeople dressed in radiant hues to honor the mystical event.

Over the years, many theories emerged, attempting to unravel the secret of the Golden Blossom Rain. Some believed it to be a celestial gift, bestowed upon the town by benevolent spirits. Others attributed it to the divine touch of nature, a magical alignment of the universe.

Scientists and researchers flocked to Crestwood, armed with instruments and theories, seeking to decipher the phenomenon's origin. Yet, despite their expertise, they could not capture the essence of the Golden Blossom Rain. The petals defied examination, fading into nothingness upon contact, leaving behind only a fleeting scent of sweetness.

With each passing year, the Golden Blossom Rain continued to captivate, its allure growing stronger. People traveled from far and wide to witness the spectacle, their hearts filled with a sense of childlike wonder and the hope that the enchanting phenomenon would leave an indelible mark on their souls.

The Golden Blossom Rain reminded the townspeople of the magic that thrived within the world—the unexplained wonders that defied logic and transcended ordinary existence. It taught them to embrace the mystery, to cherish the fleeting moments of enchantment that graced their lives.

To this day, Crestwood's Golden Blossom Rain remains a captivating enigma, an unexplained phenomenon that brings the town together in awe and reverence. As the golden petals continue to shower the night sky, they remind the townspeople to embrace the extraordinary, to revel in the inexplicable, and to find beauty in the mysteries that abound.

Active Fallen Heroes

In the hallowed fields of Greenwood, a chilling phenomenon unfolded beneath the moonlit sky—a spectral army of fallen heroes, risen from their eternal rest. Their ghostly presence evoked both awe and trepidation, for these were the valiant soldiers who had fought in the harrowing battles of World War II, their spirits forever bound to the battlefields they once defended.

Decades had passed since their courageous sacrifice, yet their duty endured beyond the realm of mortality. Each night, when the clock struck midnight, the ethereal figures emerged from the shadows, clad in tattered uniforms, their spirits aglow with an otherworldly luminescence.

The fallen soldiers moved with purpose and precision, their spectral forms marching in unison across the war-torn fields. Their silent footsteps echoed hauntingly, as if echoing the battles of the past. The air crackled with an energy borne of valor and a lingering sense of duty.

Witnesses marveled at the extraordinary sight—the apparitions locked in an eternal cycle, reliving their fateful encounters. They fought their unseen foes with unwavering determination, bayonets glinting in the moonlight, phantom gunfire tearing through the silent night.

Yet, their ethereal struggles held a poignancy that transcended the realm of the living. The fallen soldiers fought not only for victory but for remembrance—for the enduring memory of their sacrifice, ensuring that the horrors of war would never be forgotten.

Those who bore witness to this spectral symphony felt a profound mix of reverence and sadness. They were reminded of the tremendous cost of war, the lives cut short, and the families left grieving. The ethereal soldiers became a testament to the lasting impact of their sacrifice—a solemn reminder to cherish the peace forged from their courage.

As dawn approached, the phantom soldiers gradually faded into the morning mist, their duty complete for another night. Their ethereal presence left an indelible mark upon the hearts of those who had the privilege of witnessing their unwavering dedication, forever etching their valor into the tapestry of history.

To this day, the fields of Greenwood bear the echoes of the fallen soldiers' steadfast spirit, their sacrifice immortalized in the midnight battles they wage. Their ethereal presence serves as a haunting reminder that the price of freedom often demands the ultimate sacrifice.

And as the world moves forward, they stand as guardians of remembrance, guiding us to honor their memory and to strive for peace, so that the battles they fought in life may find solace in eternal peace.

Otherworldly Connections: An Unlikely Encounter in the Night

Late at night, beneath the starry sky, an extraterrestrial spacecraft descended silently into the dense woods of Earth. The alien, known as Zorix, peered out from the spaceship's window, curious to explore this foreign land. Little did Zorix know that this would be an adventure like no other.

As Zorix stepped out onto the forest floor, a sudden movement caught their eye. It was a translucent figure drifting through the trees—a ghostly apparition. Zorix froze in awe, their heart racing with both fear and fascination. The ghost seemed equally startled by the alien's presence, momentarily forgetting their ethereal nature.

Before long, the two otherworldly beings exchanged glances of mutual understanding. They were both strangers in a strange land, united by their shared astonishment. But just as they began to calm down, a cackling filled the air, and a wicked figure soared across the moonlit sky—it was a witch on her broomstick.

Startled once again, Zorix and the ghost exchanged startled expressions. The supernatural encounter seemed to multiply their fears. However, their mutual trepidation brought them closer together. They realized that they were not alone in their unease.

Before they could gather their thoughts, a chilling howl pierced the night—a werewolf emerged from the shadows, its eyes gleaming with an otherworldly glow. Zorix, the ghost, and the witch huddled together, their hearts pounding in unison. They sought solace in each other's presence, finding strength in their shared vulnerability.

As the werewolf prowled nearby, an unexpected sound shattered the eerie silence. Two mischievous young boys burst forth from the bushes, laughing heartily at the spectacle they had created. Zorix, the ghost, the witch, and the werewolf jumped in fright, their fears momentarily forgotten in the face of these exuberant pranksters.

(Continued...)

Laughter soon replaced their fright as the unlikely companions realized they had all been victims of a playful ruse. Relief washed over them, and they shared a collective sigh of amusement. The alien, the ghost, the witch, and the werewolf found themselves connected through their shared experiences of fear and the joy of overcoming it.

From that night on, they forged an unexpected bond, roaming the Earth together, their encounters becoming the stuff of legends. Zorix marveled at the ethereal nature of the ghost, the witch shared ancient secrets of spellcasting, and the werewolf became a guardian of their unlikely group.

Through their encounters, they discovered that fear could bring them closer, reminding them of their shared humanity—or in Zorix's case, their shared otherworldly existence. They learned that unity and understanding could emerge even in the most unexpected circumstances, binding them together in a tapestry of the extraordinary.

And so, their adventure continued, filled with unexpected twists and turns, but always grounded in the understanding that the strangest encounters can lead to the most profound connections. Together, they embraced the mysterious, fearlessly venturing forth into the unknown, their bond strengthened by the shivers of fright that once brought them together.

Dear Reader,

As we come to the end of this collection of mind-teasing tales, we want to extend our heartfelt gratitude to you. Thank you for embarking on this journey of mystery, wonder, and unexplained phenomena. We are honored that you chose to delve into the depths of these stories and allow your imagination to wander through the realms we created.

Throughout these pages, we have strived to ignite your curiosity, spark your imagination, and leave you on the edge of your seat, pondering the mysteries that abound. We have delved into the unknown, ventured into the supernatural, and explored the recesses of the human spirit. It is our hope that these stories have brought you moments of excitement, reflection, and perhaps even a touch of enchantment.

Your willingness to join us in these mind-teasing tales is a testament to the power of storytelling. It is through shared experiences and the weaving of words that we can transport ourselves to worlds beyond our own, question the limits of our understanding, and find solace in the mysteries that surround us.

So, thank you, dear Reader, for your open mind, your willingness to explore the unexplained, and your dedication to the art of storytelling. Your presence on this journey has made it all the more meaningful. We hope these tales have left an indelible mark upon your imagination, lingering in your thoughts long after the final page is turned.

As you step back into the realm of reality, remember to keep your sense of wonder alive. Embrace the mysteries that surround us, for they are the threads that weave the tapestry of life. May these mind-teasing tales continue to ignite your imagination, and may you find joy in the wonders that lie just beyond our grasp.

Once again, thank you for your companionship on this extraordinary adventure. May your own stories be filled with magic, intrigue, and unending fascination.

With warmest regards,

Robert Tiller

Disclaimer:

The stories presented in this book are works of fiction. Any resemblance to actual persons, living or dead, or to real events, is purely coincidental. The characters, events, and situations portrayed within these stories are products of the author's imagination.

In the creation of this collection, AI technology was utilized to assist in generating certain story elements. While the AI contributed to the creative process, the final stories were crafted and shaped by human imagination and storytelling.

Every effort has been made to ensure that the stories contained herein are original and unique. No duplication or infringement of any existing works or copyrights is intended. Should any similarities occur, they are entirely coincidental.

The images provided in this book have been primarily generated using the AI tool Midjourney. Additionally, some images have been sourced from Unsplash.com, with the rights of those images belonging to the original creators. All images have been edited in some way from their original format and are a version of an original work by the author with the assistance of AI.

The author and publisher disclaim any liability, loss, or risk incurred as a consequence, directly or indirectly, of the use and application of any information or ideas presented within this book. Readers are advised to use their discretion and judgment when interpreting the content and themes portrayed in the stories.

Please note that the views and opinions expressed in these stories are solely those of the fictional characters and do not necessarily reflect the views of the author or publisher.

Enjoy the captivating tales within these pages, and let your imagination roam freely in the realms of fiction.

Robert Tiller, Author & Creator